Billy

First Published 2024
© text Jessica Dunrod, 2024
© illustrations Selom Sunu, 2024

No part of this publication may be reproduced, stored in a retrieval system, or transmitted, in any form, or by any means, electrical, mechanical, photocopying, recording or otherwise without the prior permission of the publisher or a licence permitting restricted copying.

ISBN 978-1-914303-37-1

Published by Llyfrau Broga Books, Whitchurch, Cardiff

www.broga.cymru

Billy

The Powerful Life of Billy Boston

Written by Jessica Dunrod
Illustrated by Selom Sunu

Have you ever heard of a place called Tiger Bay?

Tiger Bay is a legendary place.

A place where winners are born, and live such impressive lives that we celebrate them in our history and remember them in our books.

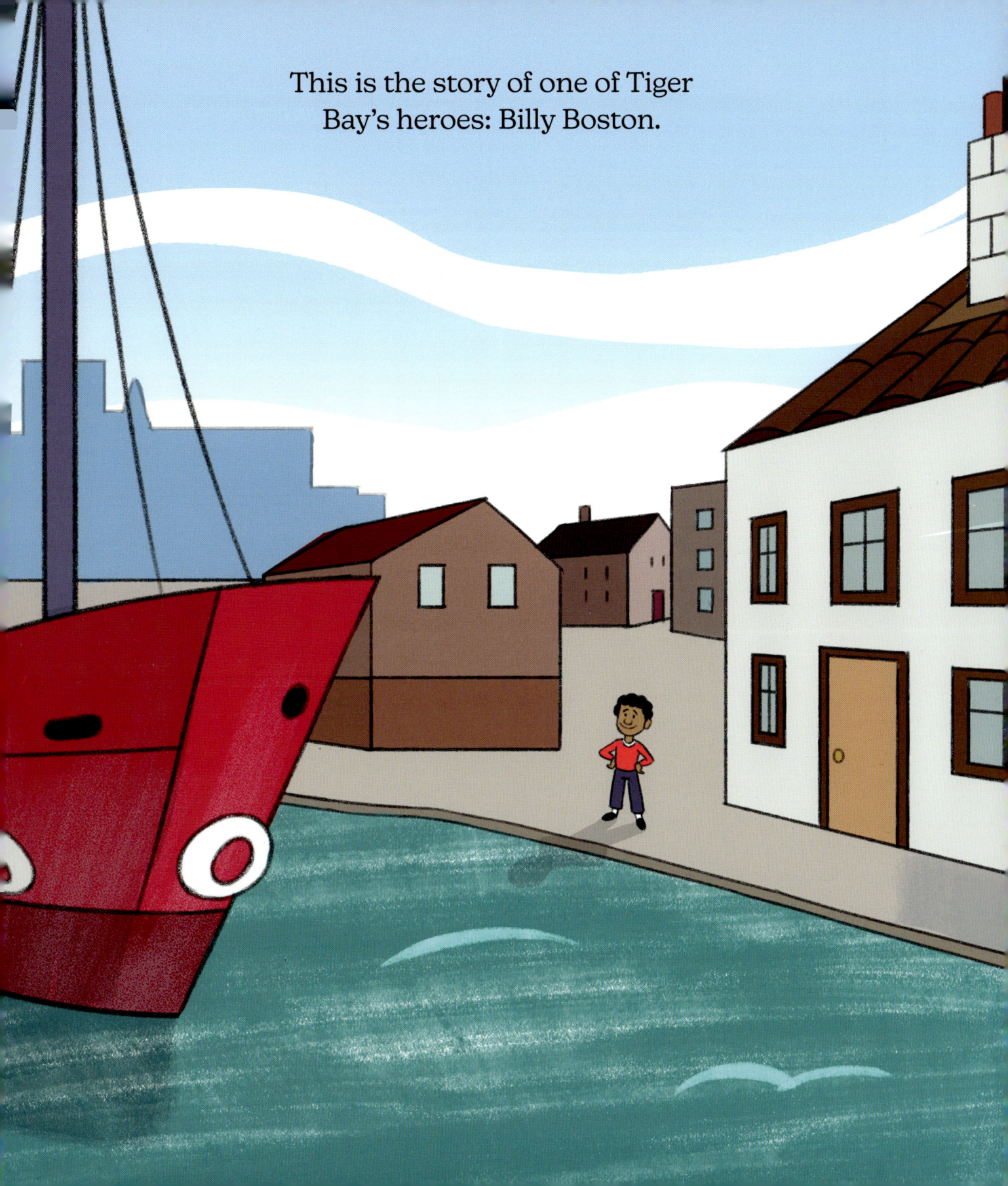
This is the story of one of Tiger Bay's heroes: Billy Boston.

William John Boston was born at number 7, Angelina Street, Tiger Bay, Cardiff, in 1934. He had ten brothers and sisters.

Everyone knew him as 'Billy'.

Billy's mum was called Nellie. Nellie's family had come from Ireland to live in Cardiff. His dad John was from Sierra Leone. He came to Cardiff to work as a sailor.

From a young age, the thing Billy loved most was holding a rugby ball in his hands ... and running!

Billy's dream was to play for Cardiff — or even Wales – one day!

When Billy ran, nobody could catch him.

He had speed. He had skill.

And he had power!

As Billy grew older, despite his talent, his power and his speed, he was ignored by many clubs. He never got to play for Cardiff, let alone Wales.

He was more than good enough, but in those days people like Billy were not treated fairly.

They were not allowed to play in some matches or with certain teams.

They were treated in this cruel way just because of the colour of their skin.

It was unfair and wrong.

Billy didn't let the unfairness stop him playing the game he loved. He joined Neath RFC and scored lots of tries.

Then, one day, he received a call from Wigan – a team from the north of England. They offered Billy a lot of money to go and play for them.

Billy didn't really want to move so far away from home, but in the end he realized that this was his chance to make a living playing rugby.

And so, after crying through the night, Billy left Cardiff on the long journey to the north of England.

From the very start, Billy was a star in Wigan.

He was fast. And skilful. And powerful!

And nobody could stop him.

Billy's position was on the wing. When he got the ball and started running, he would beat tackle after tackle ... after tackle.

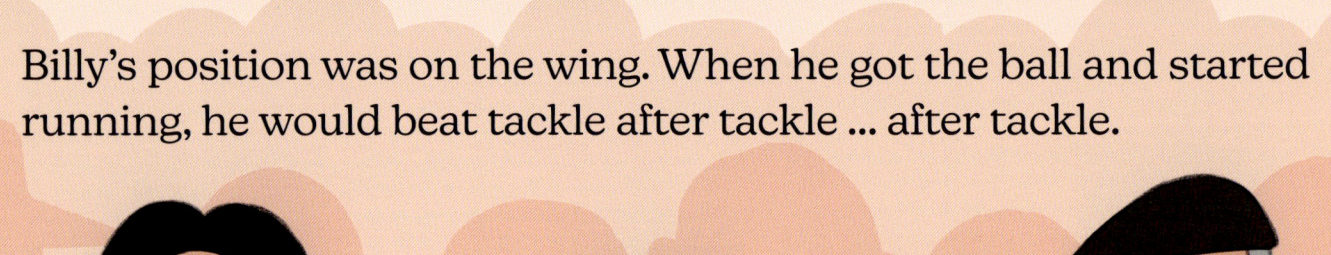

With Billy's help, Wigan won everything there was to win.

Other teams learned to fear the giant on the wing who was lightning-fast, despite being so big and strong.

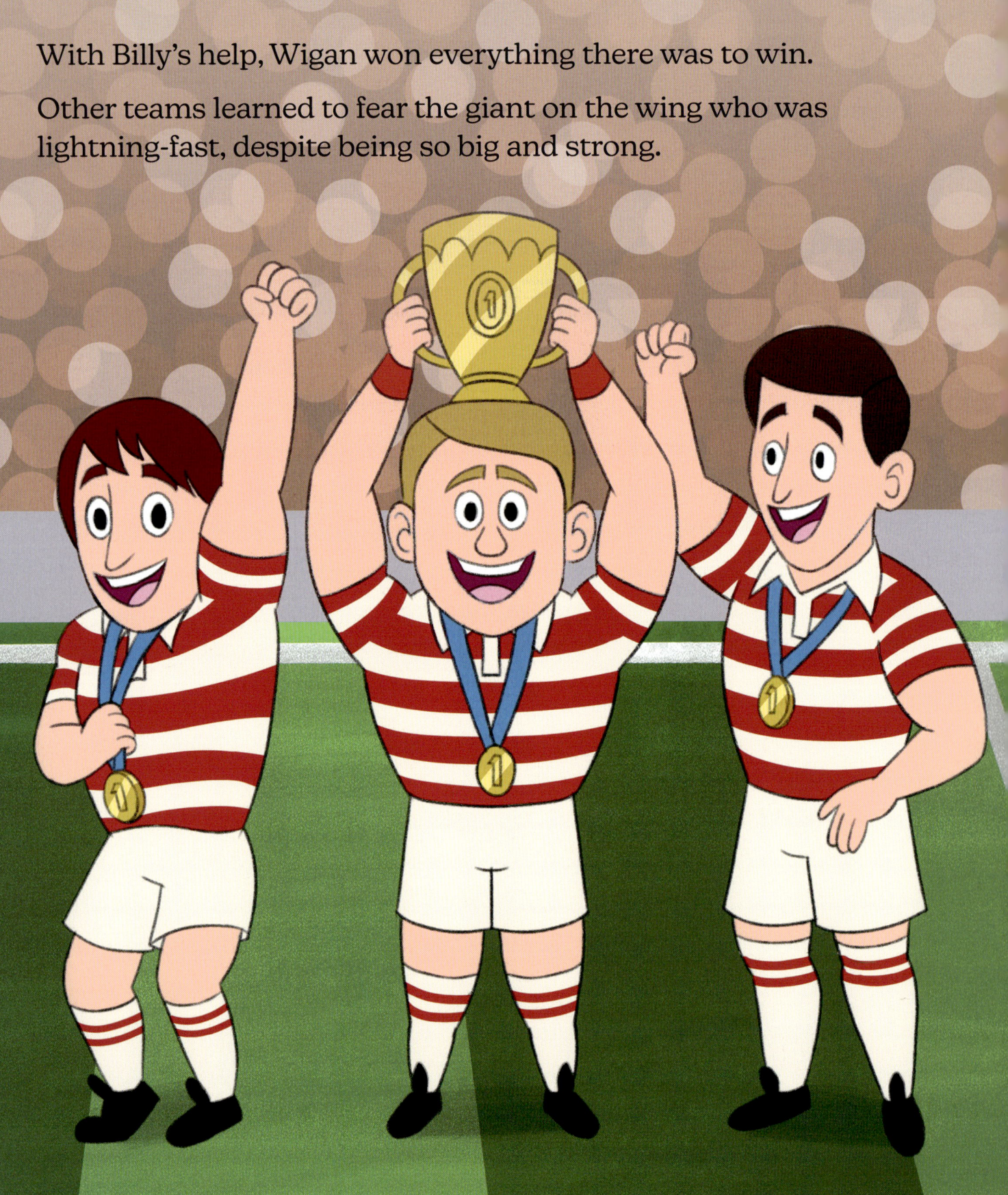

Off the field, Billy was a different character.

A kind man who was always ready to chat to anybody.

Although Wales and the WRU failed to celebrate Billy's talent, he did play 31 games for Great Britain.

He travelled around the world to play rugby and broke records when he toured Australia and New Zealand in 1954, scoring 36 tries in 18 games!

Billy was a global superstar!

By the time he finished playing, he had scored 572 tries in 562 games. Nobody else from Great Britain has ever scored as many.

The people of Wigan felt enormous love towards Billy.
They built a mighty bronze statue of him, in the town square.

He was also honoured by Queen Elizabeth, and another statue of him was put up outside Wembley Stadium in London.

In 2023 – at long last – Wales honoured Billy by unveiling his third statue, in Cardiff, near to the old Tiger Bay.

Billy's achievements were far greater than he could ever have dreamed.

Because of his talent and his determination he succeeded – despite all the barriers.

He is remembered as one of the greatest rugby players that Wales and the world have ever known.

He is a true Welsh hero, from the place that once was, and will always be, Tiger Bay.

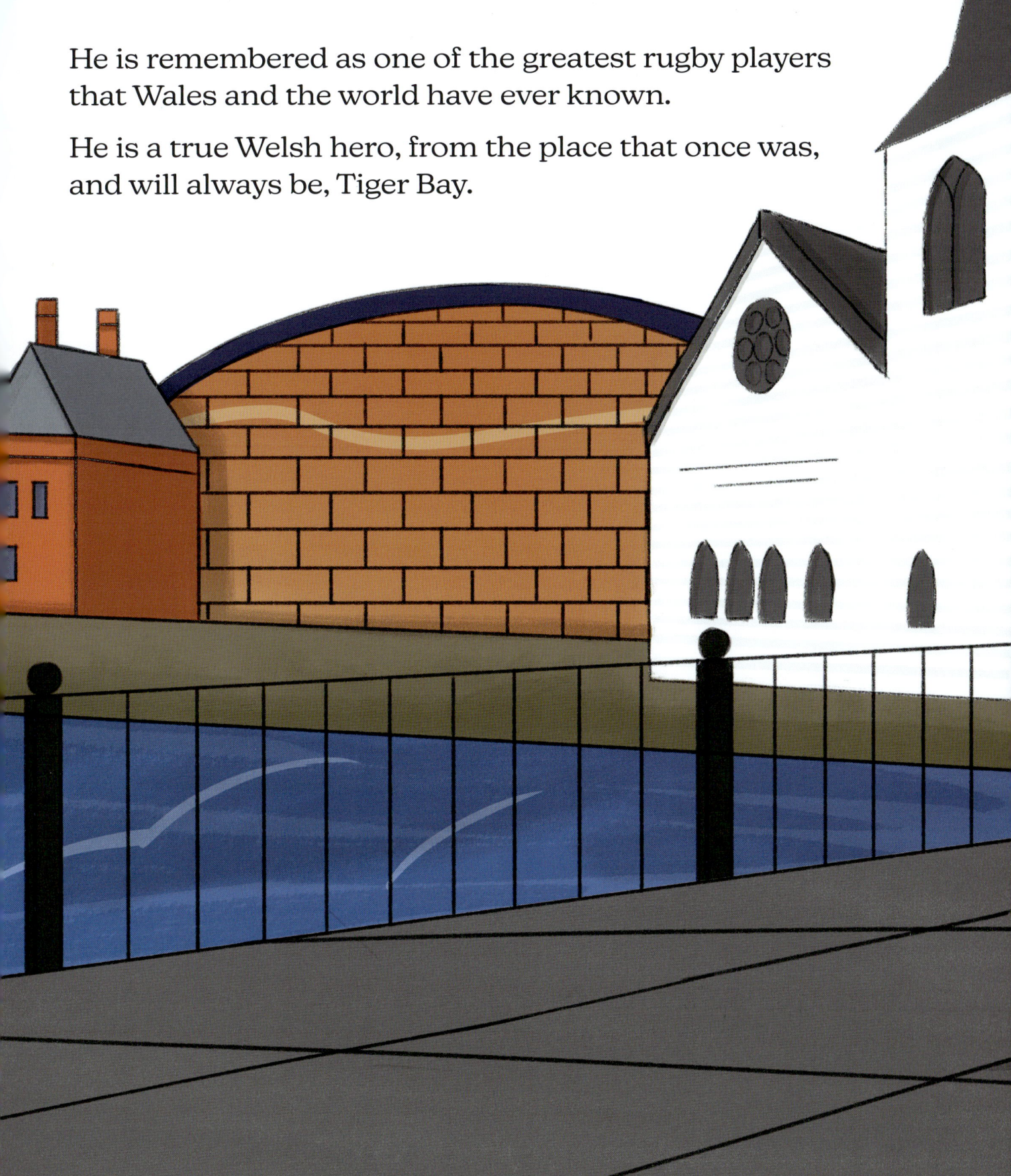

Read about more
Welsh Wonders

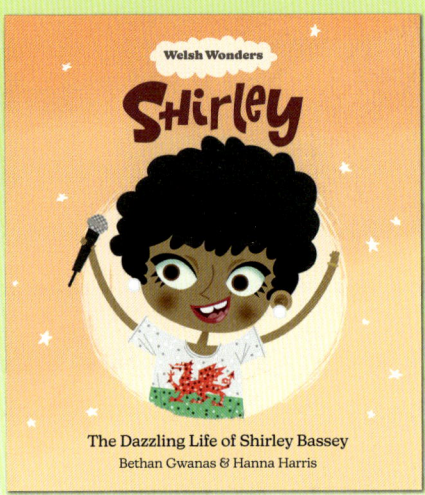

Shirley Bassey
The girl from Tiger Bay whose voice became famous around the world.

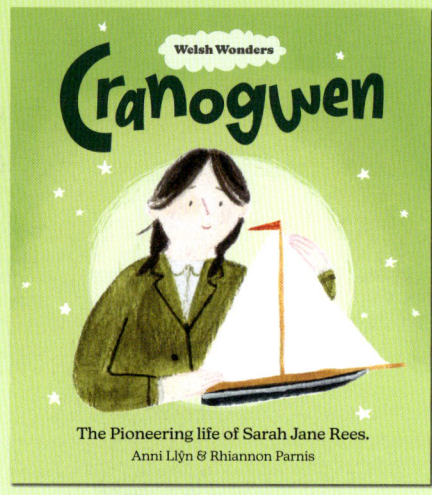

Cranogwen
Sarah Jane Rees was a sea captain, prize-winning poet, publisher, and inspiration!

Gwen John
A shy but determined girl who loved to paint and followed her dream of being a famous artist.

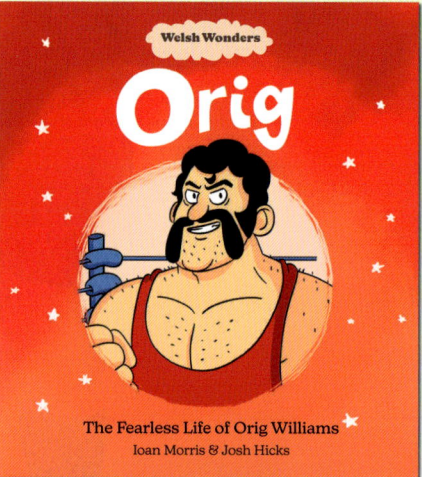

Orig Williams
The tough-guy wrestler with a heart of gold, known around the world as El Bandito!

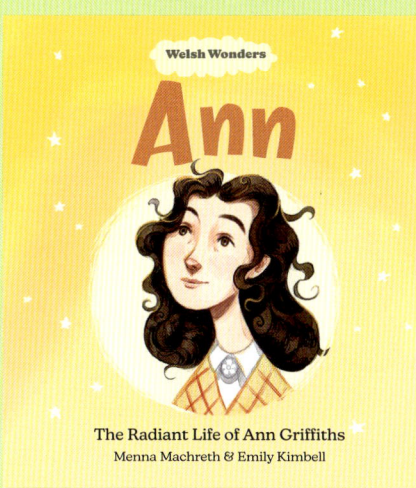

Ann Griffiths
The sensitive poet whose spiritual songs inspired millions.

Aneurin Bevan
Inspirational politician who founded the NHS and changed a nation.

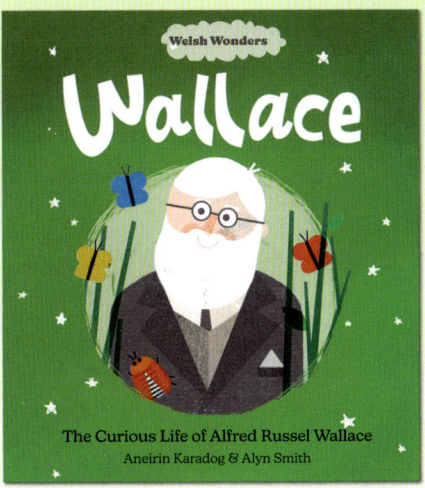

Betty Campbell
The inspirational story of Wales' first Black headteacher, who fought for equality and fairness in education.

Alfred Russel Wallace
The adventurous naturalist who travelled the world and made incredible discoveries.

Find out more about other inspiring Welsh lives – from artists and scientists to people who challenged the way things were and overcame difficulties to achieve their dreams.